Cataloging-in-Publication Data (by Cassidy Cataloging)

Otoshi, Kathryn
One / by Kathryn Otoshi -- Novato,CA: KO Kids Books, c2008.
    p. ; cm.
    ISBN: 978-09723946-4-2
    Summary: A number/color book reminding us that it just takes one to
    make everyone count.

    1. Bullying--Juvenile fiction. 2. Courage--Juvenile fiction.
    3. Colors--Juvenile fiction. 4. Counting--Juvenile fiction.
    5. [Bullies--Fiction. 6. Color--Fiction. 7. Counting--Fiction.] I. Title.

PZ7.O8775 O54 2008
[Fic]--dc22                                        0810

KO KIDS BOOKS
www.kokidsbooks.com

Distributed by Publishers Group West
www.pgw.com    1-800-788-3123

17  18  19  20  23  22  21  20

Printed in China

One

by Kathryn Otoshi

**Blue** was a quiet color.

He enjoyed looking up at the sky,

floating on the waves,

and on days he felt daring...
splashing in rain puddles.

Every once in a while he wished he could be more sunny like Yellow.

Or bright like **Green**.

More regal like **Purple**.

Or outgoing like **Orange**.

But overall, he liked being **Blue**...

except when he was with **Red**.

**Red** was a hot head.
He liked to pick on **Blue**.

"Red is a great color," he'd say. "Red is hot. Blue is not."

Then **Blue** would feel bad about being **Blue**.

Sometimes Yellow comforted Blue.

"Blue is a very nice color," she'd say.

But Yellow never said that in front of Red.

She never said, "Stop picking on Blue!"

**Green**, **Purple** and **Orange**
thought **Blue** was nice too,
but they never told **Red** to stop either.

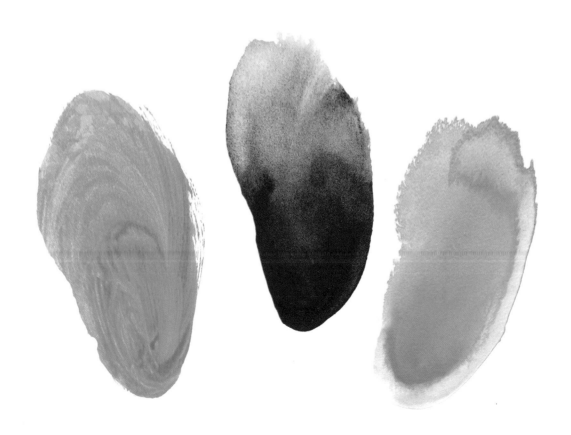

Every time **Red** said something mean
and no one spoke up, he got...

and **bigger...**

**bigger...**

and **BIGGER...**

Soon **Red** grew so big that *everyone* was afraid of him.

*No one* dared stop him.

**Red** picked on *all* the colors.

Then everyone felt...a little **blue**.

Until **One** came.

He had a different shape with bold strokes and squared corners.

He was funny.

He made the colors laugh.

**Red** saw this and got very hot.
"Stop laughing!" he told Yellow.
"Stop laughing!" he told **Green**.
"Stop laughing!" he told **Purple** and Orange.

And they did.

**Red** rolled up to **One**.

"Stop laughing!" he told him.

But **One** stood up straight like an arrow and said, *"No."*

**Red** was mad, but **One** wouldn't budge. So **Red** rolled away.

**One** turned to the colors and said,
"If someone is mean and picks on me,
I, for **One**, stand up and say, *No.*"

Then **Yellow** felt brave and said, "Me TWO!"

**Green** agreed and said, "Me **THREE**!"

Then **Purple** became **FOUR**.

And **Orange** became **FIVE**.

**Blue** saw the colors change.
He wanted to **count.**

**Red** grew red hot. He felt left out.
He grew **hotter** and **hotter** and HOTTER.

**Red** raced over to **Blue** and said what he always did.
**"Red is HOT. Blue is NOT."**

But this time **Blue** stood up tall and became...**SIX**!

"Red can be really **HOT**," he said, "but Blue can be super **COOL**."

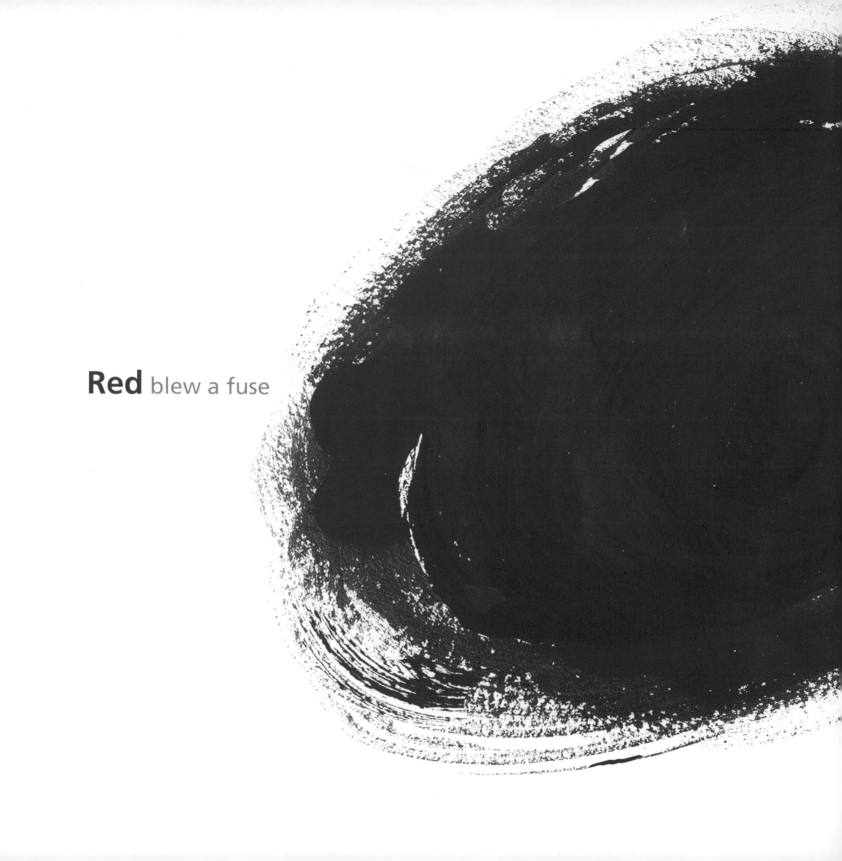

**Red** blew a fuse

and tried to roll over **Blue**!

Seeing them standing tall, made **Red** feel...

**very...**

very...

very small.

Then **Red** turned even redder, and began rolling away.

**Blue** called out,
"Can Red be hot...
**AND** Blue be cool?"

**Red** stopped in his tracks.

"Red can count too," said One.

**Red** rocked and rolled and turned into....**SEVEN**!

## "*Everyone* **counts!**" they shouted.

Then **Red** laughed and joined the fun.

Sometimes it just takes One.